3.58

THINKING ABOUT
COLORS

JESSICA JENKINS

DUTTON CHILDREN'S BOOKS
NEW YORK

rose
red

flame
red

stop-sign
red

strawberry
red

raspberry
red

poppy
red

RED

Red is the first color in my paint box
because red is for redheads like me.

Red is also
for passion...

and for the roses
Joe gives Denise.

Ouch! Watch for thorns.
Blood is red, too.

ruby red   rust red   cardinal red   crimson red   cherry red   brick red   scarlet red   blood red

When people say they see red, that means they are angry. A bull gets angry when he sees a matador's red cape.

Beware!
Red often signals danger.

But red is also the color of the Red Cross, a group that helps rescue people all over the world in emergencies.

RED SKY AT NIGHT

lemon yellow · honey yellow · mustard yellow · golden yellow · sand yellow · sun yellow · pumpkin yellow

YELLOW AND ORANGE

What about yellow and orange?
They make me think of...

spring daffodils
and summer buttercups,

autumn pumpkins,
leaves, and bonfires.

Did you know that long ago
people stuck oranges full of cloves
to make pomanders?

They looked pretty
and smelled sweet.

Someone might call me yellow
for not standing up to the monster.
That means I'm a coward.
(It's not a nice thing to say.)

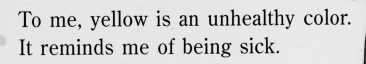

To me, yellow is an unhealthy color.
It reminds me of being sick.

Personally, I think yellow is
a lovely, sunshiny, happy color.

That's because you have a
heart of gold, Joe.

ALL AT ONCE I SAW A CROWD,

A HOST OF GOLDEN DAFFODILS.

sap green

crocodile green

lime green

slime green

spinach green

pea green

GREEN

Green is for...

green thumbs!

(People who grow things have them.)

It's not fair.
I wish I could grow things.

Rebecca is feeling green with envy. Jealousy is sometimes called the green-eyed monster!

| | mint green | olive green | sea green | aqua green | booger green | toad green | apple green | turquoise green | emerald green | dragon green |

Being green also means caring
about the planet where we live.
For example...

not picking wildflowers
(or there won't be any left)

saving paper
(to save trees)

returning empty bottles
(so they can be recycled)

avoiding aerosol sprays
(because they can hurt the sky).

PEOPLE WHO LIVE IN THE RAIN FOREST DEPEND

ANIMALS

ON TREES FOR THEIR FOOD AND SHELTER.

DO, TOO.

cornflower
blue

cobalt
blue

electric
blue

ultramarine
blue

royal
blue

BLUE

Blue is a rich and royal color.

Look, everyone—
I am the queen!
Royal blue is for the queen to wear,
because the royal family is blue-blooded.

I'm wearing my blue tights.
They keep me from turning
blue with cold.

Prussian blue   midnight blue   bruise blue   navy blue   arctic blue   indigo blue

Did you know that there is a type of music called the blues?

I know. It was invented by African-Americans. They sang the blues when they were...

sad

lonely

nostalgic

melancholy

That must have been how Picasso was feeling in his Blue Period....

PICASSO WAS A FAMOUS ARTIST. WHEN HE WAS

SAD, HIS PAINTINGS SHOWED HIS FEELINGS.

cyclamen
pink

cotton-candy
pink

blush
pink

bubble-gum
pink

lobster
pink

PINK

Pinks are flowers
that make Joe happy.

I think
I might be
in love.

Now Joe is turning pink!
He's blushing!

He's a shy pink.

coral
pink

blossom
pink

shocking
pink

lipstick
pink

tropical
pink

powder-puff
pink

grapefruit
pink

champagne
pink

Love feels pink.

It puts you in the pink of health!

PINK

SALMON

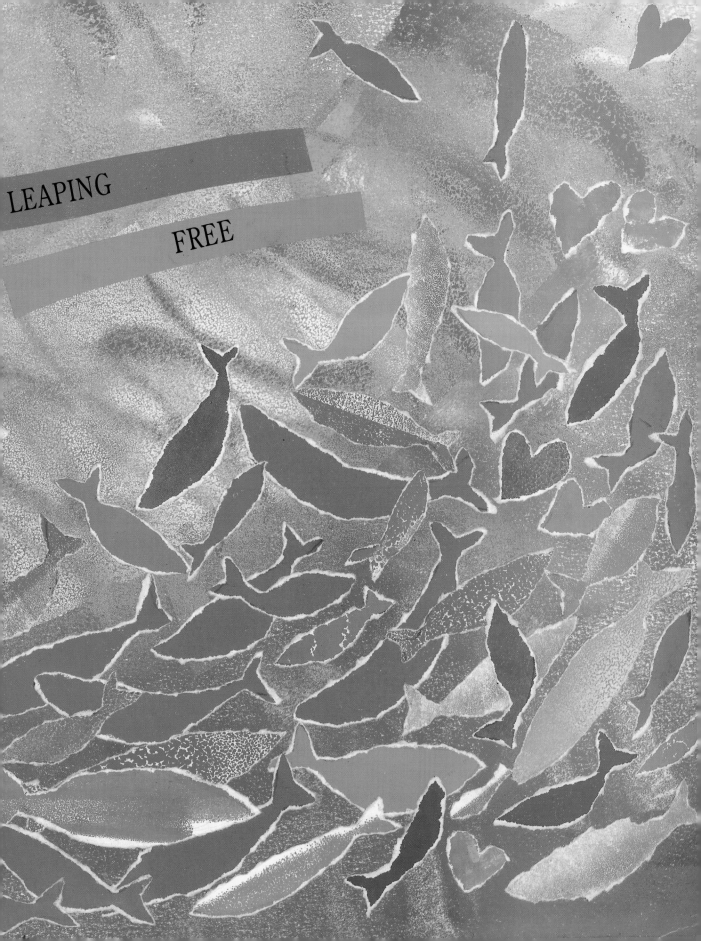

LEAPING
FREE

tar
black

coal
black

panther
black

jet
black

raven
black

ink
black

velvet
black

ebon[y]
blac[k]

BLACK

Black feels stylish.

We like dressing up
in black. It's...

trendy

Let me
try it.

beautiful

elegant

sophisticated

Black is a strong color.

I am black
and Simon is white.

But we're
all the same
inside.

BLACK AND WHITE

for Jane and Sam

CIP Data is available.

First published in the United States 1992 by
Dutton Children's Books,
a division of Penguin Books USA Inc.
375 Hudson Street, New York, New York 10014

Originally published in Great Britain 1991 by
Hutchinson Children's Books, an imprint of the
Random Century Group Ltd

First American Edition   Printed in Hong Kong
10 9 8 7 6 5 4 3 2 1
ISBN 0-525-44908-6